Merry Christmas 1996
to Cathy:
May you be able to
use & enjoy this book
purchased in Iceland ~
for a very special
Early Childhood major!

Love,
Sue ~

1st printing 1985
Reprinted 1993
ISBN 9979-3-0547-9

Prentsmiðjan ODDI Ltd.

flowers
ON THE
roof

INGIBJÖRG SIGURÐARDÓTTIR

Illustrated by
BRIAN PILKINGTON

Translation: Julian Meldon D'Arcy

MÁL OG MENNING

Shall I tell you about a granny I know? She's a really strange old lady, and so full of life! Very different from my own granny. Her real name is Gunnjona, but I always call her Granny Gunn.

Before she moved into our block of flats she used to live in the country. Her farmhouse had tiny little windows and the roof was covered with grass. Granny Gunn once showed me a picture of her farmhouse. It was just like a doll's house. And there were flowers growing on the roof!

Granny Gunn had lived all on her own there. She never got bored or lonely though because she had so many animals to play with; a cow, seven hens, two sheep, and a cat.

Granny Gunn was very lucky, she never really had to go to the shops. She got milk from her cow, eggs from her hens, and wool for her knitting from the sheep. She also had a big garden in which she grew all kinds of vegetables. Granny Gunn also knew how to make her own cream, butter, and cheese out of the milk. I think she can do almost anything!

Granny Gunn told me that one day she had become ill on the farm. This was very unlucky, because there was nobody else around to look after the animals.

She tried to make herself better by making medicines out of the herbs she picked in the countryside. But she still didn't get well, so she had to call the doctor and ask him to come and have a look at her. Perhaps he wouldn't mind feeding the hens for her as well? The cow was mooing right outside the window, so the doctor wouldn't have to go far to milk her. Granny Gunn was beginning to feel better already!

The doctor was a long time coming as he lived so far away, but at last he arrived. When he'd finished feeding the hens and milking the cow he came in to examine Granny Gunn.

She wasn't seriously ill though.

"Still, you should move into town, you know," the doctor had said. "It's not very wise to live here all alone. Your cow can't phone for me if you break your leg out in the yard!"

"I can look after myself!" Granny Gunn answered, quite offended. But then she calmed down. She pretended to be tired and closed her eyes for a moment. Maybe it would be fun to live in town, she thought. Lots of fun!

"All right!" said Granny Gunn suddenly, startling the doctor. "I'll move into town."

*H*ave you ever had to move? You have to pack all your books and toys into boxes and carry everything out into a big van – and all the furniture, too. It's a lot of hard work, I can tell you!

But it didn't take Granny Gunn long to pack. She didn't have very many things, you see. She had to sell her farm first, of course. And then Granny Gunn's cousin in town used the money to buy her an apartment in our block of flats.

But what could she do about the animals? She couldn't take them to town with her, could she? Luckily, the people on the next farm kindly said that they would look after them. It was still very difficult for Granny Gunn to say goodbye to them. She was so sad that in the end she decided she must take Robert with her, that's her cat!

Then she ordered a van and was soon on her way to her new home. She was very excited and so looking forward to seeing the town.

I was very excited, too! I couldn't wait to see who was going to move into the apartment opposite to ours. Perhaps there would be some kids … But it was Granny Gunn. Still, at least she had a cat!

That's me in the red trousers.

Granny Gunn wasn't too happy when she looked round her new flat.

"This is just dreadful!" she said. "The walls are all smooth and white. And just look at those windows! They're far too big!" She became very quiet.

"I'm off back home!" she said.

This was a really strange old lady. And so naughty! But then she suddenly gave a little scream. The cat had jumped out of the window.

"Don't worry," I said. "It's only jumped out onto the balcony. Look, you can get out through this door."

Granny Gunn rushed past me onto the balcony.

*B*ut when Granny Gunn came out onto the balcony, she forgot all about her cat. The balcony was so big, and she could see the mountains far away and even a bit of the sea. Granny Gunn crouched down so that she couldn't see any of the rooftops — only the mountains and the sky.
"Ah! Now I feel as if I'm back home in the country," she said. And then she stood up.
"And now I'm back in town!"
I thought that was rather clever, so I tried it, too. When Granny Gunn had finished arranging all her furniture and things, she started watering her flowers.
"Wow! What a lot of flowers you've got," I said.
"Nonsense!" said Granny Gunn. "You haven't seen anything yet, my dear! We'll need an awful lot of flowers to fill up this arctic waste," she said, looking round the apartment.
The next time I came to see her, she'd got all kinds of seeds and bulbs, and even pips from oranges and apples, to plant in her flowerpots.

"Well, that didn't take long," she said. "What can I do now?"

"Would you like to come for a swim?" I asked.

"Ready when you are, my dear!" she replied.

Granny Gunn wanted to see something new in town every day. I think we saw everything! The tractor exhibition, the National Museum, and all sorts of things. I liked going to the theatre best.

Once when I came to Granny Gunn's she'd bought herself a very strange present.

"I've always wanted a saxophone," she said. "And I'm going to learn how to play it, too!"

But today Granny Gunn looked very unhappy, even though she has a saxophone.

"I'm just going to sit here all day and sulk," she said.

I thought she was maybe homesick for her little farm.

"Are you bored because all your animals are so far away?"

"I do rather miss them," she sighed.

"Then why don't you go and fetch them?" I asked. "You live all on your own, so you've got plenty of room for the hens in the spare bedroom."

Granny Gunn squinted at me and gave me a funny grin.

"What a clever little rascal you are!" she said. She picked up her saxophone and started clowning around. She made the most awful noise! She's such great fun!

There was no one at home when I came to visit her the next day. Granny Gunn had taken the bus out into the country. She was going to get back rather late, so I had to try very hard to stay awake.

Very late in the evening I heard a strange cackling sound coming up the stairs. Of course! The hens had been too frightened to go in the lift!

Mum allowed me to help Granny Gunn and feed the hens. She was very glad to have my help, for they were terribly excited and noisy. Their cackling was enough to drive anyone crazy.

"Stop making such a hullabaloo!" shouted Granny Gunn. They slowly settled down in her chest of drawers and went to sleep.

Robert the cat must be happy to see the hens again. He doesn't want to get too close to them all the same.

Granny Gunn was also very happy to have her hens with her again. Now she really had plenty to do! She made some steps for them from the window of their room onto the balcony. They had their own special exit because she didn't want them to come through the living room. Sometimes, when Granny Gunn and I were sitting out on the balcony, she would close her eyes and go off into a world of her own. She never listened to anything I said when she was daydreaming.

"I feel as if I'm back home," she said one day. " The hens are cackling all around me, and if I open my eyes just a little bit, I can easily imagine that the mountains I see are those near my farm. All that's missing is the smell of earth and grass." Then she suddenly opened her eyes wide and sat up.

"Shall I tell you something?" she asked, staring straight at me.

"What?" I said, full of excitement.

"We're going to make a vegetable garden!"

Granny Gunn knocked at our door very early the following morning.
"Come on!" she said. "You must come downtown with me! We have to buy wood and nails and all the other things we need."
We came back home with a whole pile of stuff and immediately started making boxes. Then we filled the boxes with soil and some hen droppings. I thought it very strange to put hen droppings where the vegetables would grow, but Granny Gunn said it made great fertiliser.
She let me sow the carrot, lettuce, and cabbage seeds. She sowed the cauliflower and parsley seeds. Then she planted rhubarbs and strawberries and many other things.
She had also bought a Christmas tree which we planted. And I can decorate it at Christmas!
When the plants started to grow we had to pick out all the chickweed. I was going to throw it away, but Granny Gunn wouldn't hear of it.
"Hold your horses!" she said. "We can eat that!"
It tasted really good, too.

At last we could rest and take it easy.
Granny Gunn gave me a piece of cream
cake with berries in it. There's nothing I like better!
We looked proudly at our vegetable garden and
tucked into more cream cake.
"The only sad thing," said Granny Gunn, "is that the
garden can now look after itself."
"What are you going to do next?" I asked.
She stared straight back at me with that merry
twinkle in her eyes. I felt all excited once more.
Granny Gunn had clearly thought of something new.
"Well now," she said. "Don't you think it would be
rather nice to have some grass on the roof? I think
we'll have to go downtown again tomorrow!"
And that's exactly what we did.
When we got home Granny Gunn carried all the
pieces of turf up onto the roof. She laid them out
carefully, and fixed them so that they wouldn't fall
off the edge. I was longing to climb up and help her,
but she wouldn't let me.
"Only grannies are allowed on the roof!" she said.

Granny Gunn is always busy now. And so am I.
She has to cut all the grass on the roof,
and I have to put all the hay in a barrel.
"Why don't you just throw it away?" I asked.
"That's my little secret!" replied Granny Gunn.
It's so much fun being with her that I almost forget to go
home! Being on her balcony is just like being
out in the country. And me and my friends can play
hide-and-seek and cowboys and indians in her
apartment. It's just like a real jungle!

Granny Gunn is nearly always happy now. She's made a bit of countryside here in the town. So now she lives both on a farm and in an apartment! Isn't she lucky!

She's now as fond of her rooftop garden as her old farm. And there are flowers growing on the roof once more.

Granny Gunn is not like anyone else I know. She can do anything! There's only one thing which bothers her now. How is she going to get the cow into the lift?